Bobbi
the Bouncy Castle
Fairy

To Nikita, with love

Special thanks to
Rachel Elliot

ORCHARD BOOKS

First published in Great Britain in 2018 by The Watts Publishing Group

1 3 5 7 9 10 8 6 4 2

© 2018 Rainbow Magic Limited.
© 2018 HIT Entertainment Limited.
Illustrations © Orchard Books 2018

HiT entertainment

A CIP catalogue record for this book is available from the British Library.

ISBN 978 1 40834 957 1

Printed and bound in Great Britain by CPI Group (UK) Ltd, Croydon, CR0 4YY

Orchard Books
An imprint of Hachette Children's Group
Part of The Watts Publishing Group Limited
Carmelite House, 50 Victoria Embankment, London EC4Y 0DZ

An Hachette UK Company
www.hachette.co.uk
www.hachettechildrens.co.uk

Bobbi
the Bouncy Castle
Fairy

by Daisy Meadows

ORCHARD

www.rainbowmagic.co.uk

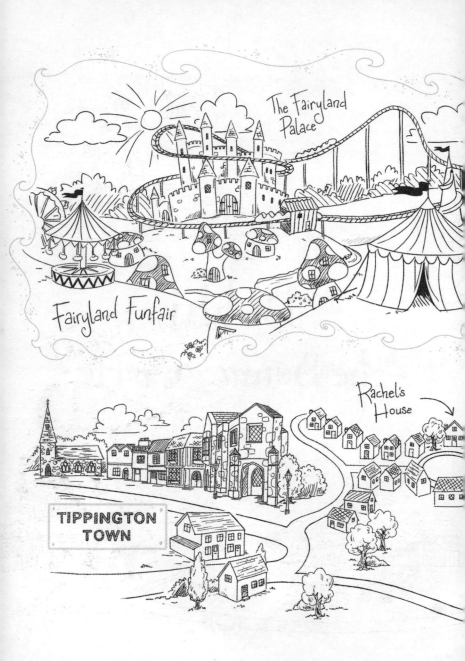

The Fairyland Palace

Fairyland Funfair

Rachel's House

TIPPINGTON TOWN

Jack Frost's Spell

I want a funfair just for me!
(I'll let in goblins, grudgingly.)
With stolen keyrings in my hand,
I'll spoil the fun the fairies planned.

Their rides will stop, their stalls will fail,
Their food will all turn sour and stale.
I'll make the goblins squeal and smirk.
This time my plan is going to work!

Contents

Goblins with Bounce

"Helter-skelter, toffee apples, toasted sandwiches, merry-go-round, big wheel," said Kirsty Tate, checking each thing off on her fingers. "It's been a super morning. What shall we do next?"

She was lying in the grass, side by side with her best friend, Rachel Walker. They were on the playing field of

Rachel's school in Tippington, where the Fernandos' Fabulous Funfair was in full swing. Matilda and Georgia Fernando came to join them.

"Would you like to go on the bouncy castle?" Georgia asked.

Rachel and Kirsty had met the Fernando twins the day before. Their parents ran the funfair, and all four girls had been enjoying it together.

"That's a great idea," said Rachel, sitting up at once.

"How about a bouncing competition?" said Matilda. "Let's see who can bounce the highest."

The girls scrambled to their feet and linked arms.

"Thank you for inviting me to stay with you this weekend," Kirsty said

to Rachel as they walked towards the woods at the edge of the school playing field.

"I couldn't enjoy it as much if you weren't here," said Rachel, smiling at her.

Georgia pointed to some trees ahead.

"The bouncy castle is just over there," she said.

"Those children must have just been bouncing on it," said Matilda.

A crowd of children was walking towards them. But as they got closer, the girls saw that the children looked very unhappy.

"I can't believe it," Rachel heard one of the boys say in a disappointed voice.

"What's a funfair without a bouncy castle?"

"That doesn't sound very good," said Rachel.

The girls started to run, and they

soon reached the place where the bouncy castle was supposed to be. They stopped and stared at a huge heap of crumpled-up purple plastic. The castle was deflated.

"No one could bounce on this," said Georgia with a groan. "No wonder those children were disappointed."

"We'd better go and tell Mum and Dad," said Matilda. "Hopefully they'll be able to sort it out. We'll catch up with you later on."

Matilda and Georgia hurried away. Rachel looked down and let out a cry of surprise.

"Look there," she said. "Under one of the castle turrets."

The purple plastic was glowing. Golden sparkles appeared at the edges of the crumpled plastic.

"That's magic," said Kirsty, darting forwards. "Help me lift the corner."

The girls lifted the heavy plastic in their hands and heaved it upwards. The magical light grew brighter, and a tiny fairy fluttered out.

"It's Bobbi the Bouncy Castle Fairy,"

said Rachel. "Bobbi, it's wonderful to see you here. Do you have news about your magical key ring?"

Bobbi twirled around them, smiling and waving. She had flowing, pale-blonde hair, a light-pink skirt that floated around her ankles and gauzy wings that shimmered as if they had been dipped in gold.

"It's wonderful to see you too," she

said. "Rachel, Kirsty, my key ring is the only one that Jack Frost still has, and he's hiding it as cleverly as he can. I need your help if I am going to be able to get it back in time. I have to make sure that all bouncy castles are as fun and bouncy as can be."

"We're always ready to help our fairy friends," said Kirsty. "We promised you that we would help you all, and we won't let you down."

She and Rachel knew that the rest of the Funfair Fairies were back in Fairyland, working hard to get ready for the Fairyland Summer Fair that evening. The day before, Jack Frost had stolen the magical key rings that belonged to the Funfair Fairies, hoping to spoil their celebrations. Without the key rings, the

Funfair Fairies could not make rides and games fun. Jack Frost was too busy planning his own funfair to care. He was going to keep it for himself and the goblins, so that no one else would be able to join in the fun.

"The Fairyland Summer Fair will be ruined if I can't get my key ring back," said Bobbi.

"So will funfairs everywhere," said Rachel, "including this one. The Fernandos have worked so hard to make this weekend perfect. We mustn't let Jack Frost and his pesky goblins spoil everything for them."

"But where shall we start looking for my key ring?" Bobbi asked.

"How about over there?" said Kirsty. She pointed to some trees further along the edge of the playing field.

"Why there?" Rachel asked.

"Just keep your eyes on those trees for a moment," said

Kirsty, with a smile.

Rachel and Bobbi stared at the trees, and then gasped. Three figures rose over the treetops for a moment and then fell out of sight.

"Did I really see that?" said Rachel, rubbing her eyes.

"Look, there they are again," said Kirsty. "They're bouncing on something."

"They've got very big feet," Bobbi remarked.

"And they're green," said Rachel. "Oh my goodness, they're goblins!"

The Fairies Fail

"Hurry behind a tree," said Bobbi at once. "I'll turn you into fairies and then we can all go and find out what the goblins are up to."

Rachel and Kirsty slipped behind a broad oak tree. Bobbi perched on a branch above them and waved her wand.

Golden-tipped white feathers floated
from the wand and drifted down on to
the girls, brushing against their hair and
skin. In the blink of an eye, Rachel and
Kirsty were tiny fairies, fluttering beside
the branch where Bobbi was sitting. They
hugged her, and then flew upwards until
they saw the goblins bouncing on the
other side of the line of trees.

"Let's go as fast as we can," said
Rachel.

Side by side, the three fairies zoomed
through the bright-blue sky. They slowed
down when they reached the trees.
Peering through the rustling leaves, they
saw another bouncy castle. This one was
working perfectly.

"It looks exactly like Jack Frost's
Castle," said Kirsty under her breath.

Rachel and Kirsty had never seen
a bigger, more splendid bouncy
castle. It had six different rooms
to bounce in, which were reached over
battlement walls or through round
windows. One of the rooms was filled
with bright-green sponge balls, which

the goblins were hurling at each other as
hard as they could in between bounces.
Another room was lined with climbing
walls, and a third had a steep slide
leading from the window to thick mats at
the bottom.

"This place is amazing," said
Rachel. "Listen, the goblins are saying

something."

"We're the kings of the castle," the goblins were chanting as they bounced.

"Except Jack Frost!" added the smallest goblin in a squeaky voice.

The other goblins pelted him with sponge balls and carried on bouncing. They went higher and higher above the trees, doing somersaults and back flips in the air. Each of them was wearing bright-green tracksuit bottoms and a matching T-shirt.

"I can't see any sign of a key ring," said Kirsty.

"We're too far away," said Rachel. "We'll have to get closer."

She fluttered forwards through their leafy hiding place, and Kirsty and Bobbi followed her. *WHOOSH!* A green sponge ball suddenly whizzed over their heads.

"Watch out!" Bobbi cried.

The fairies darted sideways as another ball came hurtling towards them. The goblins had spotted them, and were grabbing handfuls of balls as they bounced, ready to throw.

"Get them!" the smallest goblin

squawked. "Down with pesky fairies! Up
with amazing Jack Frost!"

At first, the fairies were only thinking
about dodging the balls. But the goblins
didn't have very good aim, and it was
easy to avoid being hit. Kirsty noticed
that the goblin who was bouncing
highest had a crown drawn on his head
in black marker pen.

"Look at the best
bouncer," she
called out to
Bobbi. "I bet he's
the one who has
your magical
key ring."

Bobbi stared at
the goblin as he turned
somersaults in the air.

27

"There's something silver just peeking out of his trouser pocket," she said after a moment. "I think it's my key ring."

"Let's dive for it," said Rachel in a determined voice. "We might be lucky and get it."

They zoomed towards the goblin in single file, and the goblins squealed at them in fury.

"Stop!"

"Go away!"

"Get them!"

The sponge balls came flying at them so quickly that there was no chance of dodging them. They were hit by ball after ball and sent spinning through the air until they were too dizzy to fly straight.

"Go down," called Rachel. "We have to land and take cover."

They dived down to the
ground and landed in a
panting heap next to a tree.
A squirrel darted out of
their way in alarm.

"I'm sorry to startle
you," Bobbi called
after him as he ran
up the tree.

The squirrel stopped
and stared at them
from the safety of a

29

low, leafy branch.

"We'll never get close enough to take the key ring from that goblin's pocket," said Kirsty.

"Not while we're fairies," Rachel agreed. "But maybe there's a way we can do it as humans. Bobbi, please can you turn us back into our normal selves? I've had an idea."

A Squirrel and a Surprise

Bobbi waved her wand, and instantly
the girls were human again. The squirrel
gave a surprised squeak and disappeared
among the highest leafy branches.
Rachel walked over to the bouncy castle
and watched the goblins bouncing.

"What's your idea?" asked Kirsty,
hurrying to join her best friend.

Bobbi hovered between them, and Rachel smiled.

"Goblins like a bit of competition," she said in a low voice. "What if they had a bouncing competition? Jumping really high might be enough to jiggle the key ring out of the goblin's pocket."

"Fingers crossed," said Kirsty, smiling. "We'll all have to be ready to dive for it."

Bobbi nodded, and Rachel stepped forward.

"You're all really good bouncers," she called out to the goblins. "It's hard to tell which one of you is the best."

"Me!" shouted all the goblins at once.

They glared at each other and started squabbling in mid-air.

"There's an easy way to settle this," Rachel shouted over the loud, angry squawks. "Have a bouncing competition. Whoever bounces highest must be the best."

"It'll be me!" whooped the goblin with the crown drawn on his head.

He jumped higher and higher, pumping his arms and bending his legs to get as

high as he could. But the silver key ring stayed firmly in his pocket.

"I'm incredible!" he shouted as he sprang above the trees. "I can touch the clouds. I'm the best bouncer ever. I'm the best goblin ever. I'm a bouncing genius!"

"You're more like a bouncing idiot," the smallest goblin snapped.

"The key ring isn't moving," said Rachel, feeling disappointed. "Now what are we going to do?"

"I've got an idea," said Kirsty, looking up at the goblins. "Excuse me! I was enjoying your tumbling tricks earlier. You made it look so easy to do somersaults and back flips. I'd love to see some more."

"We can show you lots more," said the goblin with the crown. "Well, *I* can, anyway. I'm the best."

"We can all do somersaults and back flips," the smallest goblin remarked.

"Mine are the twistiest and the best," said the goblin with the crown. "Ner-ner-ner-ner-ner."

Still bouncing, he stuck his thumbs in his ears and waggled his fingers.

"Prove it," said Kirsty.

The goblins started to turn somersaults in the air, twisting and turning as they bounced. They threw themselves into complicated shapes at the top of the bounce, trying to do the splits and star jumps in the air. The girls

oohed and ahhed whenever one of the
goblins did an impressive turn or landed
extremely neatly.

Just then, the goblin with the crown did
his biggest bounce yet. He somersaulted
once ... twice ... three times ... and on the

third spin the girls saw something small and silver slip out of his tracksuit pocket.

"The key ring," said Kirsty in a thrilled whisper.

The silver key ring sparkled in the sunshine as it fell. It bounced on the castle floor, spinning this way and that as the castle moved. It was flung into the air every time one of the goblins bounced near to it.

"We have to get it before one of the goblins notices," Rachel whispered.

"Leave it to me," said Bobbi.

Zigzagging between the bouncing legs

of the goblins, Bobbi flew towards her key ring. She reached out for it, but at that moment one goblin's bounce sent it spinning into the air.

"I can't see it," she cried. "It's gone!"

A Nutty Reward

Kirsty looked up and saw the little squirrel sitting on a high branch. He had caught something in his paws that shone in the sunlight.

"Bobbi, fly up!" Kirsty exclaimed.

The little fairy shot straight up in the air like an arrow and fluttered in front of the squirrel.

"Please, that belongs to me," she said.

Shyly, the squirrel held out the little key ring. Bobbi took it, and it instantly shrank to fairy size.

"Thank you," she whispered.

She tapped his paws with her wand, and they were filled with the most delicious nuts he had ever seen.

"Watch out!" shouted the goblin with

the drawn-on crown. "Fairy alert!"

"You're too late," Kirsty called out.

Bobbi flew to perch on her shoulder, and the goblin stopped bouncing and slipped off the bouncy castle.

"Give that back," he shouted, his hands on his hips. "You tricked me."

"The key ring doesn't belong to you," said Rachel in a calm voice. "It is back with its rightful owner."

The goblin stamped his huge feet in a rage.

"You interfering, nosy nincompoops!" he squawked. "You've spoiled everything. Now Jack Frost can't have his funfair and we're going to get into trouble. You're a pack of meanies."

"None of us wants you to get into trouble," said Bobbi in a soft voice. "But

41

this key ring was stolen from me. I had to get it back. If Jack Frost wants to argue about it, he can come and talk to me and the other Funfair Fairies."

"Silly flapping fairy," the goblin muttered crossly.

He turned his back on them and

folded his arms across his chest. The other goblins were still whooping and bouncing. They hadn't realised what had happened.

"I think this would be a good time for us all to leave," said Bobbi with a gentle smile. "Thank you both for helping me to get my key ring back. Would you like to come with me to Fairyland and visit the Summer Fair?"

"Yes, please," said Rachel and Kirsty together.

They never missed a chance to visit

Fairyland. They also knew that however long they spent there, not a single second would pass in the human world. Bobbi raised her wand and traced circles, curls and zigzags in the air as she spoke the words of a spell. Golden fairy dust sparkled from each shape as she spoke, until the air around her was a flurry of glittering gold.

The girls closed their eyes. In the darkness they saw ribbons of rainbow light rippling towards them. Distant bells tinkled and the smell of sweet candyfloss and rich roasted chestnuts filled the air. They felt themselves shrinking to fairy size, and smiled at the familiar feeling of fairy wings trembling and unfurling.

"Open your eyes," said Bobbi.

The girls found themselves standing in the grounds of the Fairyland Palace. They looked around in wonder.

"This looks very different from the last time we were here," said Kirsty.

"Do you like it?" asked Bobbi.

The last time Rachel and Kirsty had been here, the Funfair Fairies had asked for their help to get the key rings back from Jack Frost. The Summer Fair had been built, but it hadn't been open. Now, the rollercoaster that wound around the

turrets was filled with fairies, all squealing
in delight. The sparkling dodgem cars
that whizzed around the grounds all had
giggling passengers. Fairies were running,
skipping and fluttering in every direction,
holding balloons, munching on toffee
apples and lollipops, and adding to the
fun with their own magic.

"It's incredible," said Rachel with a
smile. "We love it."

"There's Sianne the
Butterfly Fairy," said
Kirsty, waving.
Sianne waved
back, with
butterflies of every
colour dancing
around her. Fizz the
Fireworks Fairy was

handing out sparklers, and the sky above the funfair was filled with every bird and

flying creature the girls could imagine, from dragons and firebirds to swans, owls and parrots.

Each fairy had a different pattern painted on her face, and every pattern matched the thing that they most cared for.

"Welcome to Fairyland," said a kind, familiar voice behind them.

Unexpected Guests

Rachel and Kirsty spun around to find Queen Titania and King Oberon smiling at them. The girls curtsied at once.

"Thank you for everything you have done to make today a success," said Queen Titania. "Without you, there wouldn't be a Summer Fair this year."

"You're just in time for the grand opening of the giant Ferris wheel," said

King Oberon. "We are hoping that you will join the Funfair Fairies for the first ride, as our guests of honour."

"Oh, yes please!" said Kirsty.

The queen and king swept through the funfair to the sound of trumpets. Fairies lined the way, waving and cheering.

Rachel and Kirsty hurried along behind them, glancing at all the exciting stalls, rides and games on either side. Everything was sparkling and colourful. Even the helter-skelter was studded with jewels.

"There's the Ferris wheel," said Rachel, gazing up at the largest ride in the funfair. "Wow!"

It was the biggest, brightest and most glittery Ferris wheel they had ever seen. The other Funfair Fairies were standing beside it, and they curtsied to the queen and king and then fluttered over to hug Rachel and Kirsty.

"I'm so glad that you're here in time to have the first ride on the Ferris wheel," said Rae.

"It's incredible," said Kirsty.

"The spokes are made of rose gold," said Bobbi.

"We used seashells for the seats, dipped in moonbeams to make them shine," said Fatima.

"Lucy the Diamond Fairy gave us diamond flakes to decorate

the rim of the wheel," said Paloma. "When night falls, the Ferris wheel will shine like a star."

Just then, a hush fell over the excited crowd of fairies. Queen Titania was standing in front of the Ferris wheel.

"I'm delighted to see so many of you enjoying our Summer Fair this year," she said. "The Funfair Fairies have outdone themselves. But a special mention must go to our friends Rachel and Kirsty. Without them, the funfair would have been a disaster. Once again, our human friends have come to our aid. Please give

Rachel, Kirsty and the Funfair Fairies a tremendous Fairyland cheer. Thanks to them, funfairs everywhere will be fun for everyone."

"Hip hip hooray!" shouted Melissa the Sports Fairy.

As the fairies cheered and clapped, the king and queen stepped into the first Ferris wheel seat. Rachel and Kirsty took

the second seat, followed by the Funfair Fairies. A band began to play somewhere in the funfair, and the wheel started to turn.

Rocking in their silvery seat, Rachel and Kirsty gazed out across the fairy funfair. They could see a vast bouncy castle in the distance, which looked almost as large as the Fairyland Palace itself. On the other side of the funfair was a large carousel, which rose into the air when it was spinning.

"Look, a swinging pirate ship," said Rachel.

"And a flying elephant ride," said Kirsty. "I can't wait to try that."

"There are waltzers, wave swingers, twisters and trampolines," Bobbi called to them from the seat behind.

"Don't forget the hall of mirrors," said Paloma. "That's my favourite. Instead of making you look silly, they're enchanted to make you look like different fairies, so you can find out how it feels to look like someone else."

"I don't know how we're going to decide what to try first," said Kirsty.

When the Ferris wheel stopped turning, all the fairies flew gently out of their seats to make room for the next passengers. Rachel and Kirsty swooped down towards the food stalls. Kirsty chose some sparkly candyfloss from Layla the Candyfloss Fairy's stall, and Rachel couldn't resist a giant rainbow-coloured lolly from Lottie the Lollipop Fairy.

"Come and try my skittles game," called Rae.

She led the girls to a long booth with skittle pins set up at one end. The skittles

were decorated with fairy faces, and each
ball was painted to look like a different
animal. After a few practice turns, Rachel
managed to knock down all the skittles.
Kirsty knocked hers down on her first
turn.

"You're a natural!" said Rae, clapping

in delight.

"Beginner's luck," said Kirsty, laughing.

"You both win a prize," said Rae.

She waved her wand, and Rachel found herself holding a delicate toy fairy made of wood. It had jointed arms and legs, with silky hair and real eyelashes. Its dress was white and dotted with miniature red rosebuds. The clothes were fastened with tiny poppers so that they could be properly played with. Kirsty had a similar fairy doll. Hers had raven-black hair and  a midnight-blue dress that was sprinkled with sparkling stars.

"Thank you," said Rachel in amazement. "They're so beautiful. How did you make them?"

But Rae didn't reply. Her smile had disappeared, and she was staring over Kirsty's shoulder. Rachel and Kirsty whirled around and gasped. Jack Frost was standing in front of the Ferris wheel with a crowd of goblins.

Two Fabulous Funfairs

Someone silenced the band, and the happy chatter of the fairies died away. Queen Titania fluttered forward and landed in front of Jack Frost.

"Welcome to our Fairyland Palace," she said in her calm, strong voice. "I hope that you are all here to enjoy

the Summer Fair and be part of the
celebrations. But you and your goblins
will be asked to leave if you cause any
trouble."

"Your fairies have been causing trouble
for my goblins for the last two days,"

Jack Frost grumbled.
"Why should I tell
them to behave
themselves?"

"The Funfair
Fairies have only
been searching
for their rightful
belongings," said
the queen. "They
have done nothing
wrong."

Jack Frost let out a

huffing noise, but said nothing. His frown grew deeper.

"Can't we just stay for a bit?" one of the goblins pleaded in a squeaky voice. "It looks brilliant here."

Rachel saw Jack Frost's eyes darting left and right. He was taking in all the sights of the funfair, and she could tell that he felt excited.

"All right," he said, as if he really didn't want to say yes. "Just this once, we'll do what the queen says. But I'm only agreeing to it because I am a kind and generous ruler. Say thank you."

"THANK YOU!" the goblins shouted.

Jack Frost clapped his hands over his ears as the goblins scattered through the funfair. Then a smile spread over his face and he raced after them. The queen

raised her hand and the music started up
again.

Soon, the fairies had almost forgotten
that Jack Frost and his goblins were there.
They were all having such a good time
that they forgot to cause any trouble.
The next time Rachel and Kirsty saw
Jack Frost, he was strolling along with a

lollipop in one hand and a candy cane in the other. His mouth twitched when he saw them.

"I think that was almost a real smile," said Kirsty in wonder.

"Are you having a good time?" Rachel asked him. The almost-real smile made her feel brave.

Jack Frost cleared his throat as if he were a little embarrassed.

"I have to admit," he said, "those fairies really know how to put on a show. My funfair at the Ice Castle isn't quite as ... er ..."

"Fun?" Kirsty suggested.

Jack Frost nodded. "Maybe their magical key rings didn't contain all their funfair magic," he said. "I expect that's why mine wasn't as good."

"It isn't magic that makes this funfair so good," Kirsty said. "You wanted to keep your funfair for yourself, but the fairies want everyone to have fun."

"Why should that make a difference?" Jack Frost asked in surprise.

"Because sharing things with your friends makes them twice as good," said Bobbi, coming up behind Rachel and Kirsty with the other Funfair Fairies.

Jack Frost shrugged and wandered off towards the dodgems.

"We've come to say goodbye," said Rae. "It's getting late, and it's time to send you home."

Rachel and Kirsty hugged their new fairy friends goodbye.

"Thank you for everything," said Paloma. "I hope we see you again soon."

Bobbi flicked her wand. The fairy
funfair disappeared in a whirl of sparkles,
and Rachel and Kirsty were back at
the Fernandos' Fabulous Funfair in
Tippington. Blinking fairy dust out
of their eyes, they saw that they were
standing in the place where the goblin
bouncy castle had been. Matilda and
Georgia were running towards them

across the grass.

"It's all fixed," Matilda called.

"What about that bouncing competition?" Georgia added. "We'll race you there!"

A few seconds later, all four girls arrived at the purple bouncy castle. This time it was fully inflated and ready for fun. They kicked off their shoes and clambered on. Soon they were bouncing side by side, their hair flying up as they jumped.

"This is so much fun," said Rachel to Kirsty after a few minutes. "But I can't bounce any more. After spending so long running around the Fairyland funfair, my legs are aching."

"Mine too," said Kirsty, laughing. "We tried our best, but I think Matilda and

Georgia have won this competition."

They climbed off the bouncy castle, laughing and gasping for breath. Matilda and Georgia were still bouncing high.

"We should give them a prize for winning the bouncing competition," said Kirsty.

"How about the toy fairies that we

won in Fairyland?" said Rachel as she
put on her shoes.

"That's a brilliant idea," said Rachel.

When the twins climbed off the bouncy
castle, Rachel and Kirsty presented them
with their prizes. Matilda and Georgia
were delighted.

"I've never seen such beautiful dolls,"
said Matilda. "Are you sure you want to

give them to us?"

Rachel and Kirsty nodded.

"We know you'll give them a good home," said Kirsty.

"After all, we've got something better than toy fairies," Rachel whispered to Kirsty as the sisters were putting on their shoes. "We've got friendships with real fairies!"

"Would you like to come to our caravan and have some lemonade?" Matilda asked.

"Yes, please," said Kirsty.

Arm in arm, the four girls headed back towards the funfair. Rachel and Kirsty glanced back at the bouncy castle and exchanged a secret smile. They had shared wonderful adventures with the Funfair Fairies, and they knew that now the magical key rings were back where they belonged, they would be able to relax and enjoy the last few hours of the Fernandos' Fabulous Funfair.

"I wonder when our next fairy adventure will be," Kirsty whispered.

Rachel smiled at her.

"Soon, I hope," she said. "But whenever and wherever it comes, I know we'll be ready for it!"

The End

**Now it's time for Kirsty and
Rachel to help...**

Ellen the Explorer Fairy

Read on for a sneak peek...

"I've never had breakfast on a train
before," said Rachel Walker. "It makes
everything taste extra yummy."

She still couldn't believe that they were
halfway around the world. It was only
a day since they had left Wetherbury
and boarded an aeroplane, but it felt like
longer. Now they were sitting on a train,
speeding towards the Congo jungle.

Rachel pressed her nose against the
glass of the dining-car window. The
famous *Jungle Express* train was speeding
across a vast, flat savannah. She could see
mountains in the far distance, and blue-

white clouds swirling around their peaks. Rachel turned and smiled at her best friend, Kirsty Tate.

"I still can't believe that we're really here," said Kirsty. "My mum told me that the *Jungle Express* is one of the most famous trains in the world."

Rachel nodded and picked up a teaspoon to stir her cup of hot chocolate.

"Even the teaspoons are engraved with the *Jungle Express* emblem," she said.

The girls smiled at each other and sipped their drinks. They were the best hot chocolates either of them had ever tasted.

"Your cousin Margot is so lucky," said Kirsty. "She's only a year older than us, but she has been to some of the most amazing places on the planet."

"That's because Aunt Willow is such

a famous explorer," said Rachel. "Every school holiday, she and Margot go adventuring together. We hardly ever see them. Last year they spent the whole summer holiday in the Amazon rainforest. Dad says that the harder a place is to get to, the more Aunt Willow likes it. And this time, we actually get to join them."

"Tell me all about it again," said Kirsty with a wriggle of excitement.

"Aunt Willow has been trying to find the Lost City of the Congo for as long as I can remember," said Rachel. "Now she thinks she has found the map that will lead her there. She said it will be the discovery of a lifetime. We have to take the train to the station on the edge of the Congo jungle and meet an aeroplane that will fly us across to the river. We'll take a boat down the river to a landing place, and then trek to the Lost City."

Kirsty leaned forward over the white tablecloth, her eyes sparkling.

"It's so thrilling," she whispered. "I'm not used to such incredible things happening in the human world."

Read **Ellen the Explorer Fairy** to find out
what adventures are in store for Kirsty and Rachel!

Calling all parents, carers and teachers!
The Rainbow Magic fairies are here to help
your child enter the magical world of reading.
Whatever reading stage they are at, there's
a Rainbow Magic book for everyone!
Here is Lydia the Reading Fairy's guide to
supporting your child's journey at all levels.

Starting Out

Our Rainbow Magic Beginner Readers are perfect for first-time readers who are just beginning to develop reading skills and confidence. Approved by teachers, they contain a full range of educational levelling, as well as lively full-colour illustrations.

Developing Readers

Rainbow Magic Early Readers contain longer stories and wider vocabulary for building stamina and growing confidence. These are adaptations of our most popular Rainbow Magic stories, specially developed for younger readers in conjunction with an Early Years reading consultant, with full-colour illustrations.

Going Solo

The Rainbow Magic chapter books – a mixture of series and one-off specials – contain accessible writing to encourage your child to venture into reading independently. These highly collectible and much-loved magical stories inspire a love of reading to last a lifetime.

www.rainbowmagicbooks.co.uk

"Rainbow Magic got my daughter reading chapter books. Great sparkly covers, cute fairies and traditional stories full of magic that she found impossible to put down" - Mother of Edie (6 years)

"Florence LOVES the Rainbow Magic books. She really enjoys reading now" - Mother of Florence (6 years)

The Rainbow Magic Reading Challenge

Well done, fairy friend – you have completed the book! **This book was worth 5 points.**

See how far you have climbed on the **Reading Rainbow** opposite.

The more books you read, the more points you will get, and the closer you will be to becoming a Fairy Princess!

How to get your Reading Rainbow
1. Cut out the coin below
2. Go to the Rainbow Magic website
3. Download and print out your poster
4. Add your coin and climb up the Reading Rainbow!

There's all this and lots more at
www.rainbowmagicbooks.co.uk

You'll find activities, competitions, stories, a special newsletter and complete profiles of all the Rainbow Magic fairies. Find a fairy with your name!